Bedtime St

Rita Snowden has writ
and many others for grown-ups too.

She lives in New Zealand, where she was born, and not long ago Queen Elizabeth II awarded her the Order of the British Empire – the O.B.E. – for her work and writings.

RITA F. SNOWDEN

Bedtime Stories
and Prayers

*With illustrations
by
Eileen Armitage*

COLLINS
Fount Paperbacks

First published in Fount Paperbacks in 1979
Second Impression October 1980

© Text Rita F. Snowden 1979
© Illustrations Eileen Armitage 1979

Made and printed in Great Britain by
William Collins Sons & Co Ltd, Glasgow

THIS BOOK BELONGS TO

....

It is a happy book. Because prayers
and stories are important, they don't
have to be solemn.

This is God's world – full of jolly
people, and things to discover.

God is our heavenly Father – talking
to Him, and listening to Him, is prayer.
It can happen anywhere, at any time – but
it is best to have a special place,
and time.

So let us make a start.

R.F.S.

Contents

Part One

Sugar for the Horse

Morning by morning, as they eat their breakfast, fathers in London read the paper. One morning, among news of great happenings in the world, something very nice was printed. It was set right at the head of the column so that nobody would miss it. It wasn't about a big and important person, or a clever person, or a rich person. It wasn't about a war, or a wedding, or anything like that – for I read it myself.

It was about a little boy named Michael, making his first visit to London. Michael – whose other name was Bartlett – lived, the paper said, in a place called Wallington, down in Surrey. On his first visit to London with his father and mother, he happened to see a policeman's horse, named Dante, slip and fall outside his stable in Great Scotland Yard. Though Dante managed to struggle up again on to his feet without unseating his rider, it was a nasty thing to have happened.

Michael and his father and mother moved on presently, to see the many wonderful sights awaiting them in London, but he couldn't get Dante out of his mind. At night, when he was safely tucked up in bed, he fell to wondering how Dante was feeling, and if he was hurt. He talked about him so much that, in the morning, his father promised to write a letter to New Scotland Yard, where the London policemen have their offices, and ask about Dante.

When the letter was written, Michael added to it a small box from his toy cupboard, full of sugar-lumps 'to make the horse better', and a bar of chocolate 'for the kind rider'.

One morning soon after that, the newspaper said, a big, important-looking letter came for Michael. It was from the Senior Metropolitan Police Officer, telling him about Dante, and thanking him for caring.

It was such a surprising letter for such a small boy – such a big, important-looking letter – that somebody told the Editor of *The Times*. And although he had lots of news waiting to go into his paper, he put this little story about Michael right into the very top of a column of print. He plainly hoped that lots of people would read it – and I, for one, did. And that just shows how wise the Editor was – *for any little thing that is kind is really big and important*, and deserves a place in the newspaper.

Some of the loveliest words of Jesus – part of His Sermon on the Mount – are about things like this. Each part of

His sermon begins with the word 'blessed', which means 'happy' – 'Blessed are the merciful,' it says in one part, 'for they shall obtain mercy.' Little boys like Michael have to be told that mercy is loving, caring kindness, like he showed to Dante.

Somebody who knew about 'blessed' being 'happy', and 'mercy' being loving, caring kindness, once wrote this for us all:

Happy are they who are kind to dumb creatures, for they are the children of the Father who made all things.

Happy are they who laugh when they feel like crying, for they shall be called God's heroes.

Happy are they who forgive others quickly, for God's sunshine shall be on their faces.

Happy are they who want very much to grow up wise and good, for God is their helper.

(Anon)

The Little Bear

Once upon a time, a Dutch family settled in America. They had sons and daughters who married and had sons and daughters, and they married and had sons and daughters.

At last, one of the sons of that family became President of the United States of America. His name was Theodore Roosevelt.

He was a big man, and a good man, and he had lots of energy. He led his people in ways of peace, and they

trusted him. In his spare time he liked to travel and meet people. He liked to read books – and to write them. And he liked to go hunting in the woods.

One day, when he was hunting, he came suddenly on a little bear. It was a very little bear, and with the huntsman's dogs standing yapping on either side of it, it looked smaller than ever. It was just a baby bear, and it was frightened. It knew it couldn't get away.

When President Theodore Roosevelt – whom his friends called Teddy, for a nickname – saw the little bear, he called off the dogs, and stood by to guard it, until it could run away back into the woods.

And it ran away, and was soon safe.

But those who saw the big man and the little bear suddenly began to laugh. He looked so big, and the little

bear looked so small – but most of all they laughed at a hunter with a gun letting anything get away that he might have shot. They did not understand the sort of kindness called mercy, in the heart of their big President, and when they got out of the woods, back to where newspapermen worked, they told them the story. And they laughed in a hard, unfeeling way at what they called the President's weakness.

'Fancy,' they said, 'he could have shot it easily – and he let it get away.' And they laughed again.

Then they got one of the cartoonists – one of those clever men who draw funny pictures for the papers – to draw a picture of the big man, President 'Teddy' Roosevelt, with a gun in his hand, turning his dogs off the little bear to allow it to go back into the woods. And lots of people who saw it in the paper, laughed too. But lots didn't, because they knew what mercy was, and how important it was. They had read in their Bible this wonderful thing: 'What doth the Lord require of thee, but to do justly, and to *love mercy*, and to walk humbly with thy God.' (It is in the Old Testament book of Micah, chapter 6, verse 8.)

Just about that time, the toy shops all over the land were beginning to sell little toy bears for children to play with. They were cosy, friendly little bears – but they hadn't a name for them. So when they heard the story of the

President – 'Teddy' Roosevelt – and the little bear in the woods, they called them 'Teddy-bears'. And Teddy-bears they have been ever since.

Perhaps you have one of your own. Now it will seem to you nicer than ever, because it is a reminder of a big man whose heart was big enough to show mercy.

Three Secrets

One morning, a lady named Mrs Palmer got into the train for the big city. It was a very hot morning, even in the country, and she knew that when she got up to the stone and brick buildings of the big city where there was hardly any breeze, it would be worse.

Mrs Palmer wasn't going to shop; she was going to see some children – a whole hall full of children. Because they knew she was coming, they were all there when she got there. The children were very poor, and had nowhere nice to play, so they carried with them the babies they had to mind, and spent the whole morning in the hall together listening to music, painting on large pieces of paper, and listening to stories. Always Mrs Palmer began by asking them, 'What shall I tell you about in my story today?' This day, one little girl said quickly, 'Tell us about life.' That was a hard thing to do. But just then, another little girl with a fat baby on her knee, said, 'Well, tell us how to be happy.'

Mrs Palmer looked at them all for a moment, then she said, 'Well, I will give you my three rules for being happy; and mind, you must all promise to keep them for a week, and not skip a single day.'

They all promised. 'The first rule,' said Mrs Palmer, 'is that you learn by heart something every day – something lovely. It needn't be much – just three or four words from the Bible, or a pretty poem. Do you understand?'

One little girl jumped up from the corner and said, 'I know. You want us to remember something we'd be glad to remember if we went blind.'

'Yes,' said Mrs Palmer, 'that's it, exactly.

'And the second rule is, Look for something pretty every

day – and don't skip a single day. A leaf, a flower, a cloud – you can all find something. And keep looking at it long enough to say: "Isn't it beautiful!"

'My third rule is – now mind you don't skip a day – do something for somebody every day. Help with the babies, run the messages, something.'

They all promised.

At the end of the week, on a day hotter than ever, Mrs Palmer was walking along a narrow street up in the city, when suddenly somebody grabbed her arm. She looked down, and a little voice said, 'I done it!'

'Done what?' asked Mrs Palmer, because her thoughts were far away.

'What you told us,' said the little happy child, 'and I never skipped a single day neither.'

'Tell me all about it,' said Mrs Palmer. Then they stood and talked about it there in the narrow street.

'Well,' said the little girl, 'it was awful hard for a start. It was all right when I could go out in the park. But one day it rained, and the baby had a cold, and I couldn't go out, and I thought I was going to skip. I was standing at the window, wondering and wondering what beautiful thing I could see in such an unhappy wet day; and then all of a sudden –' and here her little face lit up with a smile as she told about it – 'I saw a sparrow taking a bath in the gutter that goes round the top of the house, and he had black feathers round his neck that shone like a neck-tie, and he was handsome.'

It was the first time Mrs Palmer had heard of a sparrow being called handsome, but she believed it and hoped that one day she would see such a sight.

'And then there was another day,' said the little child, 'and I thought I was going to skip. The baby was sick once more, and I couldn't go out –' and then a smile danced over her face – 'what do you think? I saw the baby's hair.'

'Saw the baby's hair?' said Mrs Palmer.

'Yes, I saw the baby's hair,' she said. 'And a little bit

of sun came in through the window just at that minute, and oh, it was beautiful!'

And she picked up the baby from the side of the street where she had set him down while they were talking. 'Look, isn't it beautiful,' she said, 'when the sun shines on

it?' And it was.

And next week when Mrs Palmer went again to the hall
in the big city, there were ten times as many children, and
ten times as many babies, and they all had a jolly time
telling of the lovely things they had remembered – one

lovely thing every day; and the lovely things they had seen – one lovely thing every day; and the lovely things they had done for other people – one lovely thing every day.

A Little Church Mouse

When suddenly you see a little mouse, what do you do — hop up on a chair? Or let out a little scream for help? Lots of quite big people are afraid of mice — I wonder why?

Miss Rose Fyleman, who wrote many happy poems for children, wrote one about mice. She said:

> I think mice
> Are rather nice.
>> Their tails are long,
>> Their faces small,
>> They haven't any
>> Chins at all.
>> Their ears are pink,
>> Their teeth are white,
>> They run about
>> The house at night.
>> They nibble things
>> They shouldn't touch
>> And no one seems
>> to like them much.
> But I think mice
> Are nice!

A jolly little poem! But I wonder how many feel that way?

A while ago, I met 'a little church mouse'. Actually he lives in a big church, a cathedral. Liverpool Cathedral is one of the greatest in England, with a wonderful, great tower. It stands on the top of a hill. The part where the people meet to worship is made without stone pillars as most cathedrals have, so that the people can get a clear view during the service.

There are lovely things in Liverpool Cathedral – lovely coloured windows with pictures in them made of red glass like rubies, gold glass like the sun, and green glass like the fields on which the children play in springtime. And there is a great organ with voices like the wind in the trees, and the clear song of birds, and the sound of many waters. There are beautiful carvings in stone, that craftsmen have taken a long time to make. Some of them are to mark the last resting places of great men and women, with words to tell what wonderful people they were.

One of them calls to mind the Earl of Derby, who was a great man. On his tomb is a model of the cathedral which serves him as a pillow. In one corner of it there is a hole, just big enough to put your finger in. That is where I met the little church mouse. He lives inside that little hole – and if you put your finger in, you can just touch the tip of his little cold nose. He is a little stone mouse. So he doesn't run about at night and nibble things he

shouldn't. Lots of people who pass through the great cathedral don't find him, because they don't even know where to look for him.

Now why have the builders put him there I wonder, on that rich man's tomb? I think to tell us all a very wonderful thing: that in God's house, the cathedral, those who are 'as poor as a church mouse' are welcome, along with those who are as rich as the Earl of Derby. That's what four words in the New Testament mean: '*God has no favourites.*' (You can find these wonderful words in the book of Acts, chapter 10, verse 34, in Moffatt's translation.) All of us may come, for all are welcome!

Never, Never Too Busy

Do you like your name? How did you get it? There was probably a lot of talk between your mother and your father, your aunties and your uncles. It is often that way. And when the little baby is a royal princess, there is likely to be more discussion.

But that wasn't so of a little princess born in the beautiful Greek city of Athens. Cannon boomed out, and guns flashed from warships riding out at sea, the day she was born, to tell everyone within hearing the good news.

And as soon as could be, her grandfather, King George I of Greece, and her grandmother, Queen Olga, went upstairs to the big room where her mother held the little baby in her arms. Everyone was very happy. And when the tall king looked down at the little new princess, he said, 'I suggest you call her Marina. She was one of the best-loved of all the Greek saints, you know.' And that was done. When one of our English princesses heard, she wrote to say, 'I think it is one of the prettiest names I ever heard.'

And it was a name that became greatly loved in England – for one day, when little Marina was grown up, she was to go to live in England, and to marry the King's son, the Duke of Kent. She was beautiful, and her heart was full of loving-kindness – and everybody loved Princess Marina.

I want to tell you a story about her, when she was little. She still lived in Athens then, with her two sisters, her dolls and her story-books, in the care of her parents. She had a loved English governess named 'Foxy', who gave her lessons when she was old enough, and did lots of other things to make her happy.

Like all little children, Marina had a settled bedtime; but when it came – like most little children – she begged to stay up just a little longer. One time, she gave 'Foxy' her

excuse. You'll never guess it, I'm sure; so I'll tell you what it was. Said she, 'Lots of other little girls are going to bed just now. God must be terribly busy listening to all their prayers. If I go to bed later on, the rush will be over, and God will have more time to listen to me.'

A quaint excuse! Though all her life long God was very real, and very dear to Princess Marina, and the older she grew, the more she came to learn about Him.

And one of the most important things, of course, was that God is never too busy to answer His earth-children one by one. 'He loves us each one,' said a wise man named

Augustine, 'as if there were but one of us to love.' And
that is still true. No one – little Princess Marina, or you, or
anyone anywhere – can ever get lost in the crowd.

Jesus reminded us all of that, when one day a sick lady,
hiding in the crowd, touched His garment when He was
on earth. 'Who touched Me?' He asked His disciples.
'Master, the crowds are all around you pressing hard,' they

said. But Jesus said, '*Somebody touched Me.*' (The story is told in Mark's Gospel, chapter 5, verses 25 to 34.)

And when we pray to His Heavenly Father, and ours, we can't ever hide from Him. He loves to answer us one by one. Little Princess Marina learned this, too, as she grew up – and it made her very, very happy, beautiful and true.

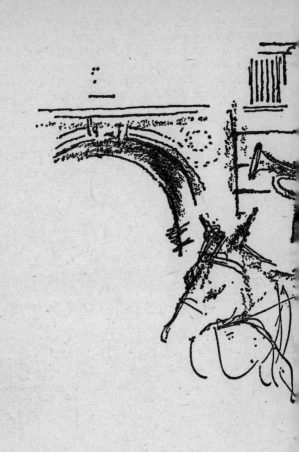

The Best Prize

It was an exciting day for the boys and girls and big people of Stockholm. Especially for one little girl. She was only seven, but she would never forget that day. Crowds lined the streets eager to catch a glimpse of the King of Sweden, as he came out from his palace. He lived in their beautiful city of Stockholm, and on this day every year, just before Christmas, he came out to take part in a great celebration. They saw him at other times, too, but this was special. Waiting in the city – where the lake met the sea, with the sun sparkling on the water and on the islands – were many people who had come a long way to be there. For the fame of Stockholm and its Nobel Prize was known in many parts of the world.

Alfred Nobel had been born in that beautiful city; and although he had only been to school for two terms, he had been taught at home by tutors, and had become a wise man. He had also become a very rich one. But often he was very lonely, because his health was not good. More than that, he had never married, so he had no boys and girls of his own.

But one day – thinking of all these things – a wonderful idea came to him. Each year he would give what should be called The Nobel Prize, divided into five parts. And five years after he died, it was first given.

Each Nobel Prize was made up of a gold medal, a fine piece of parchment with important writing and the name of the prize-winner, and also a big sum of money. From year to year, a group of clever men were given the task of deciding who most deserved the Prize. To win it, it was necessary to do something very special for the world.

Among the winners, on that lovely day in 1952 that the

little girl would never forget, was a very clever American scientist. His name was Professor Selman Wakeman. Now what had he done? I must tell you. He had found out a very useful drug called *streptomycin*. (It's a hard word for some of us to spell, even to say, but it stands for a drug that now helps doctors bring healing to lots and lots of sick people all round the world. So its discoverer, Professor Wakeman, deserved the Nobel Prize.)

And on that happy day, the King of Sweden gave it to him, in sight of all the people – a gold medal, a fine piece of parchment with beautiful printing and his name on it, and a big sum of money. And, of course, he was honoured to have the Prize.

But then something else happened; unexpected by the crowds, the little girl of seven came forward, and, presenting the clever professor with a bunch of flowers, she thanked him for saving her life. She had been very, very ill, and was the first patient in all Europe on whom the new medicine had been tried. And her life had been saved.

Wasn't that a lovely, unexpected thing to happen? Certainly the crowds thought so – they clapped and cheered to show their joy. And certainly the clever professor thought so. 'This,' he said, '*means more to me than getting the great Nobel award.*'

No wonder! It was so nicely said, so unexpected, and so deeply felt.

Whenever I think of that happy day – and it's nice to think of it often – three simple words seem to jump right into my heart from the New Testament: '*Be ye thankful!*' (You can find them in your New Testament, in Colossians chapter 3, verse 15.)

You and I may never get a chance to say our thanks to a great man, with a bunch of flowers, but there are people all about us all the time who do nice things for us, important things, and they are glad to have our thanks. And, above all, God, Who gives us much, much more than even a clever prize-winner, a father or a mother, a teacher or a friend, or anybody, is glad to have our thanks. You can puzzle out your own best way of saying it to Him. One little person put her thanks to God in a poem:

Thank You for making
This world so much fun,
For making the blue skies
And the bright yellow sun,
For wee things we see
Like tadpoles and snails,
For putting the wiggle
In little dogs' tails,
Thank You, dear God,
For all of the cheer
You've put in this world —
I'm glad to be here!

(Anon)

All the Little Lights

Year by year, for Indian boys and girls and their parents who live in that part of the country called the Punjab, comes a beautiful festival. It comes when the hot sticky nights of the monsoon have given place to the long pleasant evenings before the coming of the cold nights of winter.

It is called the Festival of Diwali (Dewallee), the festival of light.

At once all the housewives are busy preparing their homes for the families to sleep indoors, instead of out. The walls are given a new plaster to freshen them up, and then redecorated with colourful drawings.

But that is not all. As the evening of Diwali draws near, the housewives take hundreds of little earthenware saucers, and fill each with a few drops of linseed oil. Then they twist little pieces of cotton wool into wicks, place them in the saucers, and set them alight. With these hundreds of tiny lights, their homes are outlined against the dark velvety night. And what a pretty sight that is!

To go down into the bazaar on Diwali night is just like walking into fairyland. All the houses have their little lights, and so, too, do all the shops, shining against the warm Indian night.

As you walk along you are sure to wonder how it is that a light so tiny can continue to burn so brightly.

But there is a secret. Look more closely, and you will see, behind the lights, a man standing with a tin of oil in his hand. He moves quietly up and down between the rows of lights, and wherever he sees one beginning to flicker, he pours in a few more drops of oil, so that the little light is replenished, and it can continue to burn brightly against the dark of the night.

And that's a wonderful secret for us to know. That is what Jesus does for us His earth-children. He calls us to let our lives shine like little lights in the world – and we try to do that. (We can read His words in our New Testament – Matthew chapter 5, verse 14: 'You are the light of the world!')

But we soon find that we cannot keep this up all by ourselves, any more than the tiny lights at Diwali. All the time – through work and play, Bible reading, and worship in church, through the beauty of the world, and the love of those about us – He must keep close to our lives, to replenish them so that they can keep on shining brightly and clearly. Without His help day by day, they would soon die, and that would be very sad.

But with His wonderful, loving help, each of us can shine through kindness and love and joy, as brightly as a little light in the Festival of Diwali.

Shiny Shoes

All nice people, big and small, like shiny shoes. Mother looks them over before we set out for school; and Teacher when we get there, before class starts. They are important, along with clean nails, knees and ears.

In some big cities, where people are walking about all the time, there are shoe-cleaners sitting on stools at street corners, with little boxes of brushes, soft cloths and polish. Each cleaner has a little place for passers-by to put a shoe that needs polishing, and then another. This costs a few pennies. In some countries this polishing job is done by small boys.

One day, two visitors were going for a long walk in a town in Portugal. There were lots of lovely things to see – beautiful buildings, and interesting things offered in shops. It was a very sunny morning and Jan and Cora Gordon, the two visitors, walked on for a long time.

At a street corner they found, again and again, a bunch of boys begging to be allowed to do their shoes. 'Look!' they cried. 'They are dusty. You don't want dusty shoes. Let us clean them!'

At last, they came to one bright-faced little boy all alone. He asked the same question. Could he clean their shoes? And this time, they decided to have them done, and the little boy got out his brushes and polishing-rags. To finish off, he took from his pocket a rag that looked as soft as velvet, and rubbed away. Soon Jan and Cora Gordon could almost see their faces in their shiny shoes, they were so beautiful.

The little boy looked up with a smile when he had finished. 'There!' he said, 'I have polished them!'

Having given him a few coins for his work, the visitors then looked at the time. They wanted to go down to see

the fishing boats before it got too late. And on they went, through the wet sand. The boats, nets and sails interested them very much – and especially the people busy working at them. Time went so quickly, so happily.

Then it was time to go back to find something to eat. Presently, they came on a clean little shop, with tables outside. They sat down, and gave their order. First of all, they each wanted a cool drink. And who should come along but the little boy with whom they had done business an hour or so earlier. He gave them a nod to show that he remembered them. Then he dropped his gaze to their shoes. At once his smile was gone. 'But your shoes,' he said, as he saw what the wet sand had done to them. 'I clean them again?'

'No,' answered Jan and Cora Gordon both together. 'We have had them cleaned once. That is enough.' But it wasn't enough for the little cleaner-boy. He got out his cloth and started in on the job. 'But I will clean them for nothing,' he said. '*I can't have my work walking about looking like that.*'

As soon as I heard of that little boy, I took an instant liking to him. I am sure Paul – Jesus's friend – would have, too. He said once. 'Whatsoever ye do, do all to the glory of God!'

When another boy, Samuel Chadwick, who later became a wonderful preacher, first started to love God, he said, 'I put my love for God into the polish on my father's shoes.' Before that, he hadn't been very particular. But when he came to serve God as his great heavenly Father, he delighted to make a good job of everything he did, in the very best way he knew – just like the little shoe-shiner in Portugal, who said, 'I will clean them for nothing. I can't have my work walking about looking like that.'

In Portugal, England, Palestine, any other place – it makes no difference. I think God gets a lot of happiness out of things like this. Don't you?

Thank-You Prayers

Thank You, God, for making this great world – and for keeping it going. I like it full of people, and creatures, and things to do. Let me be kind to all I meet, sharing my laughter, and my work and play. AMEN

Thank You, God, for all in our house. They are kind to me, and You are kind to us all. Let our home be a happy place. And let us each help to keep it that way. AMEN

God, I'm glad that You made dogs with wagging tails, and pussies to sit on steps. Help me to be kind to them.

I'm glad that You made trees and open grassy places. Thank You for seeds to grow, and for plants and flowers. AMEN

Thank You, God, for strong, clever fathers. They can do hard things. They can mend bikes and toys; they can earn money to buy things in shops, to eat and to wear. Let me never forget children who have nothing nice to eat or to wear. AMEN

Thank You, God, for the loving care of mothers – for all the things they can cook, and the things they care for. Let me be gentle as they are gentle, and kind and truthful in all that I say, ever willing to share. AMEN

O God, You are good and loving to old people. I know some. I am thinking of ...... and ...... Help all of them who have aches and pains; all in hospital waiting to get better. And help all who help them. AMEN

Thank You, God, for our everyday helpers – the baker who makes our bread, the grocer who sells us things we

need, the postman who brings us letters. Keep all these safe in their work, day after day. AMEN

Thank You, God, for pilots who fly planes, and for air-hostesses who fasten our belts. Guide the fast planes in the sky, and bring them down again safely to earth, I ask. AMEN

O God, all the men who work with motors and loud engines need Your help. Show them what to do. And guide the drivers of trains, and captains of ships. Bring them back to their homes safely. AMEN

Thank You, God, for pretty things in parks and gardens, and for pretty things at home. Let me be unselfish about the things I have. Make me ready to share my books and toys. AMEN

Thank You, God, for paints – and all the gay pictures I can make when I try. Thank You for songs, and happy dancing words – and for all I can remember when I try. AMEN

O God, my pocket is a secret place – so is my heart. But You know all that is inside, and I am glad. You long for me to be happy and friendly. Show me every day how to do new things. AMEN

Thank You, God, for clean, cool water to drink – and for some to paddle in. I love pools, rivers and the sea. Thank You for making sands to dig in, and for putting pretty shells there. And for the fish. AMEN

Thank You, God, for thinking of lambs in the spring, and for the woolly mother-sheep to care for them. Thank You for tiny leaves that freshen the trees, and for buds that burst into bright flowers. AMEN

Dear God, thank You that every day when the sun gets up, there are new things to do. Thank You for keeping me, wherever the day finds me. Show me how to be a friend to all, and a good, unselfish playmate. AMEN

O God, You have made birds and butterflies, and grasshoppers with funny ways. You have made pools for frogs, and streams for fish. You have made sun and showers, and rainbows over the smiling sky after showers. Thank You for these. AMEN

Thank You, God, for showing people how to write stories; and showing people how to put them in books. Thank You, too, for showing artists how to make the pictures. Help the book-sellers, and the librarians with their lots of books. AMEN

Thank You, God, for giving Your boys and girls and big people ripe fruits – oranges and bananas and pineapples in hot countries; plums and apples and other fruits here where we live. We love the sweet taste of them. AMEN

Thank You, God, for all manner of things which come from shops – shoes and clothes, bats and balls, bikes and skipping-ropes, and puzzles and dolls. Please comfort today all sick boys and girls unable to play. AMEN

Thank You, God, for new things to learn every day – for new games, for new lessons, and for new ways of helping

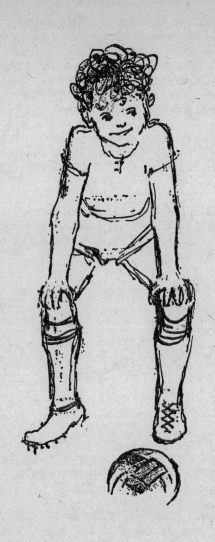

others. Thank You for sweet air, winds and sunshine; and for bathtime and bedtime when we are tired. AMEN

Thank You for songs – the songs of birds and hurrying streams; the songs of boys and girls. Some of them we sing by ourselves when we are happy; some we sing to give You joy when we come to church. AMEN

Dear God, keep safely all the babies in their homes, and help those who look after them. Please don't forget the baby pussies and puppies and birds, and tiny new leaves on the trees. AMEN

O God, it is fun to go to the zoo, and to see all the creatures You have made. Big ones, and tiny ones – they are lovely to see. Help all the helpers who care for them for You. AMEN

O God, I am glad that You sent Your dear son Jesus to our world. He was born a happy baby. He grew up to be a little boy, learning things, and later a good, kind Man, telling people about Your love. AMEN

Thank You, Father God, for the lovely stories of Jesus told in the New Testament and in church. Thank You that He wants to be my unseen friend, and to keep close to me, to make me brave. AMEN

God, keep all the preachers and teachers, and the priests and nuns everywhere. Help them when they have to travel far from home, or live in strange and dangerous places, for Jesus's sake. AMEN

Give patience, dear God, to all gardeners, who dig and rake and weed and plant seeds. Help them to mow their lawns, and keep their hedges trim. Thank You that we can all share their gardens. AMEN

Strengthen the farmers who work hard to look after the animals, and to grow crops for us. Encourage the men and women to grow fruit for the market. And save them from being greedy for high prices. AMEN

Thank You, God, for fresh air to breathe and make us strong; and for places on which to run fast. Thank You for little paths, and for roads that go on adventures. Keep us safe when we go, too. AMEN

Jesus loved the flowers and grasses, and all the birds and creatures – He knew they belonged to You. They are still Yours – help me never to forget that, because they teach me of Your love and strength and care. AMEN

It is nice, O God, that You made horses and ponies. Jesus rode on a little donkey when He was a baby; and

when He was grown-up, He rode into the city on the back of another little donkey, lent by a friend. AMEN

Thank You for Your church here where I live, and in all the round world where other people live. Thank You for all that I can now learn about the daily life and loving service of Jesus. He is my friend. AMEN

Thank You, dear God, that in this great, exciting world, so many boys and girls and big people want to be friends with Jesus, too. Some live in lands far away from here – but all are safe within Your love. AMEN

Thank You, God, for making so many different people – for lovely brown skins, and white skins, and black skins and yellow skins, they are all good. I am glad that every one is precious to You. AMEN

O God, when You send the cold mornings, with ice, frost and snow, it is fun to race to get warm, and to skate, and

make snowmen and snowballs. Keep the old people and the tiny babies warm, and safe and sound. AMEN

Thank You, heavenly Father, for bringing my birthday round each year. You know how eagerly I wait for the days to pass. Now that I am getting big, let me learn lots of new things, I pray. AMEN

This party day, all the nice food and fun with friends is mine to share. Let no unkind word spoil it. All the surprises of this day are proof of other people's loving thoughts for me. Jesus had birthdays, too, and was happy with His friends. AMEN

Thank You, God, for rides in the country, and picnics in the summertime. Thank You for green grass to play on; for trees and water and flowers. Keep us all safe on the roads as we come and go. AMEN

Thank You, God, for home and for church, for all that happens in these nice places, and for all who share things with me there. Thank You for Your strong, lasting love — and for all Jesus told us about You. AMEN

When Christmas comes round, I think of Jesus born as the little babe in the manger. I think of the bright star shining overhead, and the shepherds who came with presents. Let me offer my love now. AMEN

When Easter comes, O God, let me finish the sad story of Jesus being killed by the wicked men, with the glad story of Him rising again from His tomb, to be alive for ever more! Hurrah! AMEN

Every day, dear God, brings fresh things to learn, and fresh things to praise You for sending us. This is a wonderful world. You have made it because You love us, and like to show us Your love. AMEN

Part Two

The Doctor's Knobbly Bag

Once upon a time, there was a kind doctor, called Dr Ernest by all the boys and girls, and to them he was the most special doctor in the whole world. His real long name was Dr Ernest Ofenheim. He went to England from Vienna, in the beautiful country of Austria, to St John's Hospital in London.

St John's Hospital was a very little hospital at that time, with only thirty beds, room enough for thirty sick people. But by degrees it grew and grew and grew. And it was a very happy place to be in if one was sick.

Dr Ernest – perhaps we had better call him by his full and proper name – Dr Ernest Ofenheim – got to love the hospital and to love the sick people. And he got to love the boys and girls especially. He loved them so much that he wanted nothing so much in the whole world as to be allowed to stay at the hospital and help. He didn't even want any money – he could manage with what he had – he wanted only to help.

And he stayed at St John's Hospital helping all he could for twenty-five years, which is a very long time. And because the sick people loved him, and felt safe when he was about, they soon got better. Always he had such kind hands and such a kind heart.

There was one very special thing that he did for the boys and girls. Every week a bag was brought to the hospital. I'm sure you'd never, never guess what was in it. Every doctor carries a bag, but this wasn't an ordinary doctor's bag – it was a knobbly bag. And it only appeared once a week. (I'd better tell you what was inside it, because I'm sure you'd never guess.) It was full of pennies – every one of them bright and new and shining! And, more surprising, there were always enough to go round, so that every sick boy and girl got a bright, new, shining penny.

It was wonderful to see the Sunday smiles come creeping out when the pennies appeared – more bright and shining even than the pennies themselves from the doctor's knobbly bag. And the smiles lasted long enough to help some of the very sick boys and girls feel better.

It was such a lovely idea that the doctor kept it up to the end of his life. And when at last he died, he left a fund so that Sunday by Sunday bright, new, shining pennies could still be given to the sick children.

That was *the Doctor's Sunday gift*: every Sunday a bag full of pennies!

But wonderful as that was, *the Doctor's everyday gift* was just as wonderful – perhaps more wonderful. For his everyday gift was kindness and love and knowledge and care – all things that help to make this world bright and beautiful.

His Sunday gift wouldn't have been half so good without his everyday gift. Just as his everyday gift wouldn't have been half so good without his Sunday gift, his knobbly bag full of bright, shining pennies.

Now you each have a Sunday gift. You give it to God to help His church and His missionaries, as well as His little boys and girls who don't have nice homes of their own – you put it into the collection in church, when it comes round.

But what is your everyday gift? For a Sunday gift isn't any good without an everyday gift: kindness and love and smiling joy and gentleness.

Once, somebody who knew this wrote a little verse about it. It says:

> King of Glory, King of Peace,
> I will love Thee . . .
> Sev'n whole days, not one in seven,
> I will praise Thee!

Cats are Cats

Smut was quite a common little cat to lots of people – but not to his mistress, Mary, aged seven. To her, Smut was the most special cat anywhere. Mary loved everything about Smut – his velvet toes, his coat of fur, his amber eyes and his great big purr. And he was a clever cat, too – he could catch mice. He was a quick cat – he could catch a woolly ball. And people said he had nine lives. Mary wasn't sure about that, but she did know that he was a wonderful cat.

One day, Mary wrote down Smut's story. It wasn't a very long story – all in one sentence, without pausing for commas. It was quick like Smut himself. And the spelling was Mary's own kind of spelling.

But a famous editor, who didn't get many cat stories, printed it in his important paper *The Guardian*. So lots of people got to hear of Smut. This is how the story read: 'My cat Smut is a cleva cat at home he has four legs when he runs on top of the wall he has more legs wen he runs fast he has so meni legs I can not cownt I could tell lotsa bowt Smut, but not his legs its a misteri.'

Of course, it is not easy for anybody to write down everything about a loved cat. As a poem in a little boy's book I know, says:

> Cats are not at all like people,
>   Cats are Cats.
> People wear stockings and sweaters,
> Overcoats, mufflers and hats.
> Cats wear nothing; they lie by the fire
> For twenty-four hours if they desire.
> They do not rush out to the office,
> They do not have interminable chats . . .

> People, of course, will always be people,
> But Cats are Cats.

That's true! God made cats to have their own ways, and their own thoughts. They are not meant to be like people.

But as well as looking with amber eyes, arching furry backs, moving quickly, and purring when they are content, they can do courageous things. If we could go together to St Augustine's Church, along Watling Street in London, we could learn the story of a very courageous little cat. It's a longer story than little Mary's story of Smut that was in the newspaper – but not much. It is a story of the bad, bombing, bashing-down days of the war. The story says:

On Monday, 9 September 1940, she endured horrors and perils beyond the power of words to tell.

Shielding her kitten in a sort of recess in the house (a spot she selected only three days before . . .) she sat the whole frightful night of bombing and fire, guarding her little kitten.

The roofs and masonry exploded, the whole house blazed, four floors fell through in front of her. Fire and ruin were all around her.

Yet she stayed calm and steadfast and waited for help.

We rescued her in the early morning while the place was still burning, and by the mercy of Almighty God, she and her kitten were not only saved, but unhurt . . .

What courage God had put into the heart of that little cat! It's splendid to know about her, as about Smut. But it is still true – as the little poem says – that 'Cats are not at all like people, Cats are Cats'. God has put into the hearts of boys and girls and big people, not only courage, but the power to love Him back, as the great Father of us all; the power to worship Him in church, and in the secret places of our hearts; and to serve Him day by day, with love, all our lives long. That – for all their cleverness, quickness and courage – cats cannot do. But you and I can – and that is wonderful!

Bags of Bumble-bees

As Steven lay in the long grass a little song began to sing itself over in his mind. It wasn't a school song, or a Sunday song, or anything that he could ever remember having heard before. It was a song right out of the blue sky and the sweet air over Grandfather's farm, out of the sun and his own heart. For it was holiday time, and Steven had been watching a fine fellow go by in the tall grasses over his head, wearing a coat with a band of yellow round it. He was so long in passing, that it seemed he must be on holiday, too. It was at the end of what seemed a long time there in the sun – but it could have been only a few minutes – that the little song started in Steven's head:

> I'd like to be a bumble-bee
> 'A-bumbling' in the sun,
> With my striped furry coat on,
> And all my lessons done.
>
> I'd pick my way from flower to flower
> The whole long term-time through.
> It would be fun to 'bumble'
> Without a thing to do.

It was a very private little song, not for singing to other people, so Steven kept it to himself all summer. And it was still in his heart as term-time drew near. Then, one day he was out watching Grandfather on the farm, when what looked like the same fine fellow came by. If he wasn't the same bumble-bee, he was so like him you couldn't tell the difference.

When Grandfather saw him 'bumbling' away on the sweet full head of red clover, he exclaimed: 'Welcome

64

God's good helper!'

Steven looked up, remembering his little song – and puzzled to know what Grandfather meant. 'I've just been learning,' said Grandfather, 'how farmers like me, and scientists like you might be one day, are getting concerned in the northern parts of the world, because bumble-bees are becoming fewer. Fear that they might one day die out altogether has visited some hearts – and that's a fear too terrible to think about.'

Puzzled, Steven asked after a little silence, 'Why, Grandfather?'

And then he was told how the bumble-bee is one of the few bees in the world with a tongue long enough to reach the nectar of the red clover. 'Bumbling' from clover to clover, getting the nectar, he brings out also the pollen, and when he moves to the next flower, he leaves a little behind. So the clovers can form seeds, and those fortunate to have a soft soil in which to fall, grow, and there are lots more next year.

'Clover is very important to us farmers,' said Grandfather. 'It is one of the cows' main foods. Without clover, there would soon be less meat and milk.'

Then Grandfather went on to tell Steven an even stranger thing – about a 'bumble-bee farm'. At first, Steven thought it was another of Grandfather's little jokes; but not this time. The first 'bumble-bee farm' in the world was started in Britain, by the Botany Department of the University of South Wales and Monmouthshire, in the great Welsh city of Cardiff. It sounds an odd sort of farm, doesn't it? We may have had holidays on farms like Steven's grandfather's – cow farms; and we've heard about sheep farms – but never before about a 'bumble-bee farm'. But it's real. It is run, Steven learned, by Dr Mary Percival and her assistant at the University, Miss Patricia Morgan.

They started by going round as many gardens as they could in Cardiff, catching bumble-bees and putting them into paper bags. (Have you ever heard a bumble-bee 'bumbling' in a paper bag? Well, it's a mighty bumble.) But all went well, and they took the queen bumble-bees back to a specially prepared greenhouse, where they were introduced to male bumble-bees. In the winter, when it was cold, and the queen bumble-bees wanted to snuggle down and go to sleep, these clever ladies, Dr Percival and Miss Morgan, put them into a refrigerator. In the spring – just as they planned – the bumble-bees wakened up and started to have families of little baby bumble-bees. These were put carefully into nice little boxes, specially prepared. When anyone like Steven's grandfather suddenly began to get worried about the few bumble-bees on his farm, he could write to the bumble-bee farm at the University, and get some for his clover-fields.

Interesting, isn't it? Steven felt so. And to think he'd been reckoning that the bumble-bee 'bumbling' over the fields was just a lazy fellow, when all the time he was one of God's good helpers! You won't be surprised when I tell you that Steven never sang his little song again after that.

One day, as he found himself thinking about his own special job in the world, he came across a nice verse in his Bible which he hadn't noticed before. It said: *What soever ye do, do all to the glory of God!* (You can find it in your Bible: I Corinthians, chapter 10, verse 31.) And what a secret of happiness that is!

A Christmas Song

One day, a song danced into the heart of a little boy just ten years old. His name was Edmund, Edmund Hamilton Sears, a nice sort of sing-song name. He lived with his father and mother on a farm away up on the hills of Massachusetts, another sing-song name. It was a busy farm where everybody in the family had to help.

Each morning, before they set off, Edmund's father – who loved stories and songs and heroic deeds – read aloud to his family something out of the Bible. Little Edmund loved that: the stories of Joseph, and of David and others, the songs of the happy hearts now called Psalms, and the stories of Jesus.

Under the blue sky, about his farmwork, little Edmund had plenty of time to think over them. One day, a little song came dancing into his mind – a new song, his very own. After he had sung it over and over, his first thought was to write it down.

But that brought him a problem. Because he was out there on the hillside, he had no paper. What was he to do? Suddenly, an idea came to him. All around him, lying almost hidden in the grass, were pieces of soft white limestone. He picked up one slender piece to be his chalk, and took off his black hat to be his blackboard. And it served quite well.

That night, when he got home, little Edmund read the words of his song to his father and mother. They couldn't believe that he'd done it all by himself, it was so nice. But there and then, he wrote another verse just as good – and that proved it.

In time, growing fast, Edmund went away to boarding-school, then to college, and later still, to university. But learning, learning, learning, he never forgot to sing. For a

year he served as a missionary – sharing with people those stories he had heard his father read to the family long before. Next, he became a minister of a church – rather like your minister, teaching and helping lots of people, including boys and girls. But Edmund never forgot to write songs. It was a long, long time since he had written his very first, on his hat, but with better things to write with – pencils and paper – he wrote every song that came into his heart.

And one day, he wrote a song that was to become very famous all round the world. It was about the joy that had come into the world with the first Christmas, when the little babe was born in the manger in Bethlehem. And now lots of boys and girls, as well as big people, sing it. It says with great happiness:

It came upon the midnight clear,
    That glorious song of old,
From angels bending near the earth
    To touch their harps of gold:
'Peace on the earth, goodwill to men,
    From heaven's all-gracious King!'
The world in solemn stillness lay
    To hear the angels sing.

All about Bethlehem, and the first Christmas! After we have finished singing, we can read about it in our New Testament: Luke, chapter 2, verses 7 to 20. You might like to make up a little song of your own for Christmas!

The Sculptor and the Little Children

The sun shone in the lovely old city of Stuttgart. The people went up and down the cobbled streets – the men to their business, the women to the market, and the children to school. It was a busy city, and they were proud of it, pleasantly set amongst its wooded hills.

Most of them were too busy at their work and marketing and their schooling to know that in their city lived a man who would make it famous. He was a quiet man, a sculptor. He worked with beautiful marble and stone, chipping till his dreams came true. Day after day he worked away, and nobody came to his studio. But he did not mind. He liked to be alone. He wanted to make something so beautiful that people all over the world would be nobler for it.

First, he chiselled in stone figures from the old Greek stories, men and women. One after another, he made them, but his heart was not satisfied.

'I will lay down my chisel awhile,' he said. 'I will be quiet and read my New Testament, and surely God will give me an idea.' And He did. As Dannecker sat still in his studio, God showed him that He wanted him to do a beautiful thing.

Dannecker planned for it carefully. He checked over his simple tools, and he chose for it the finest stone in his studio. Then, with his hands steady and his eye clear, he took up his chisel.

By lunchtime there was little to show.

'But there will be more soon,' said Dannecker. 'I will work slowly and carefully. One false stroke would spoil it all. I must go slowly and carefully. Nothing must be allowed to spoil it.'

By nighttime, there was little more to show. But Dan-

necker did not mind. He read his New Testament, and prayed as he laid down his tools, thanking God for the joy of doing a beautiful thing.

And in the morning he wakened early, before the men of Stuttgart had gone to their business, or the women to their marketing, or the children to school. All that day he worked carefully and happily, and night came again. And many more days and nights passed. At last, the beautiful figure was finished.

Then Dannecker went out into the streets, and found some little children. Many wise people in Stuttgart might have thought it a foolish plan, to invite little children in to see his work. But Dannecker knew what he was doing.

The little children from the cobbled streets came into the studio. Their eyes got used to the dim light, and they stood quietly looking at the beautiful figure that he had made. At last, one of their number spoke, and Dannecker knew that what he said was what each of the children was thinking: 'He must have been a very *great* man!'

There was silence after that, and the children said, 'Goodbye!'

When they had gone, Dannecker sat a long time with his head in his hands. Then he picked up his New Testament, and read again. 'No,' he said. 'He was more than a very great man! I must do better.'

And with that, he set to work again.

After a long time, he invited the little children from the streets to come again into his studio. Again they stood silent before his work, till their eyes got used to the dim light. At last, when they had been there some minutes, Dannecker asked them what they thought of it. It was a girl who spoke this time. She said: 'He must have been a very *good* man!'

As she said it, Dannecker's eyes clouded with disappointment. He knew that he had not succeeded. So a second time the little children went back to the streets.

When they had gone, Dannecker stood a long time looking at the figure he had made, and reading his New Testament. Then he took up his chisel, and went on with his work.

Days passed, nights passed. At last, when he could do no more, he called the little children again from the streets. He watched their faces closely, as they came into his studio, and this time, to his secret joy, something unexpected happened. The boys snatched off their caps as they caught sight of the figure, and the little girls fell on their knees.

Dannecker was satisfied. All that remained to be done was to carve the name underneath his beautiful figure: 'The Divine Christ'.

Human, he knew He had been – so human that He was born at Christmas in the manger, like any other little baby; but so divine was He that the angels in heaven sang over Him. So human He had grown, that He slept tired out in Peter's little fishing boat out on the lake; but so divine was He that He rose and stopped the storm. So human was He that He died on the cross; but so divine was He, that He conquered death, and rose again, and lives now for ever more!

And that is exactly why now, in church, little boys take off their caps, or we all either bow or kneel. *Jesus is more than a great Man, more than a good Man; He is the divine Son of God!*

The Little Conceited Girl

There was once a little conceited girl called Elizabeth, and she had six sisters. One day Elizabeth and all her sisters went to church, only they didn't call it 'church', they called it 'Meeting', because their father and mother were Quakers, and that is what they called their church.

Elizabeth and her sisters sat all in a row, and Elizabeth wore purple shoes with scarlet laces, and because she thought she looked very smart in her little purple shoes and scarlet laces, she was restless. Her eyes wandered down towards her feet, and she did not think very much about what was being said in Meeting.

But when the preacher began his sermon, little conceited Elizabeth suddenly forgot all about her shoes. The words of the preacher made her think of many, who were just as dear to God as she was, who couldn't have any shoes or laces at all. And she felt that she wanted to help.

At once she gave up wearing her special shoes that made her so conceited. In the town where she lived there were lots of little boys and girls who had no chance of going to school, because they were poor. So Elizabeth, when she grew up, opened a school for them. And the children loved Elizabeth, and they loved her school.

Then she married a good man named Joseph Fry, and went to live in London. But always she was thinking about the poor people, and the unhappy people. In London there were lots of these. She went to visit them. Sometimes their houses were horrid and dark, small and dirty. Sometimes their windows wouldn't open to let in the air. Sometimes their doors wouldn't close properly, or they had no beds and had to sleep on the floors. And very often they had sick babies because they lived in such horrid houses.

Elizabeth Fry took them food and clothes and books and

medicines. Sometimes when she had tidied them up, she would say, 'I will read you a story.' And she would stop and read them one of the stories of Jesus who had changed her conceited little heart into a kind heart.

Then one day she heard about the poor people who were in prison. Many of them hadn't done very bad things at all. The prison was a horrible place, all dark and damp, full of beetles and rats, and overcrowded with people. When a poor father and mother were put in prison, they

had to take their children too, because there was nowhere
else for them to go. They didn't have real beds to sleep on
or real tables on which to have their meals, and it was all
very horrid.

Elizabeth Fry began visiting a big prison where there
were over three hundred people all crowded together. And

they were very dirty because they couldn't wash.

Soon she had them washing their hands and faces, and tidying up their hair. Soon they tidied up their prison, and Elizabeth started a school there for the little children. She said: 'They will not always be in prison. We must help them to grow up good and true. They are just as dear to God as anybody.'

She found needles and scissors and stuff, and got the mothers sewing, and in less than a year they made twenty thousand garments to wear. Wasn't th. lovely? And because they were happier and cleaner and busier, they were better behaved, and many of them were let out of prison.

Then Elizabeth went to other prisons, and started all over again. She got people to help her, and she went all over the land – and by and by, to other lands. Everywhere she went, people listened to her: great people who made the laws, and kings and queens. But nothing could make her conceited any more. People said she was the most famous woman in the world, but in her heart there was only love – love for God, and love for the people – so, of course, she couldn't be conceited any more.

The Best Song of All

Some boys and girls are good singers. They can sing the low notes, and the high notes, and all in between, strongly and sweetly. It is a joy to listen to them.

Some boys and girls who are very good singers are invited to sing on the radio. I am sure you have heard some of them.

One night, in May 1926, the voice of a very special singer came over the wireless from the BBC for the first time. Those who were lucky enough to be listening at the time were thrilled. No, it was not a boy, singing strong, clear, liquid notes; it was not a girl. It was not even a lady or a gentleman. It was a little brown bird. And as people listened – some of them lonely people far from home, some of them sick people in hospital – the joy and beauty of the song touched their hearts.

At the end of the year, when the BBC asked its listeners which song they had liked best of all that they had heard, they replied, *the song of the little brown bird* – the nightingale. It was a song, they said, that reminded them of the lovely, quiet green of the woods. And it had been all the better for being a surprise.

People have always loved the nightingale, and some have made poems about its song. I want to tell you of someone who was lame, and who loved the nightingale especially. He lived in beautiful Italy. His name was Epictetus.

He lived in a great big house, but it wasn't his house; for Epictetus, sad to say, was a slave. His master wasn't a very kind master, being hard on his slaves and pleasant only to his friends. Epictetus had another trouble, too – he was lame. But despite all this, his thoughts were free.

When he did not have to wait on his master, he would hobble as best he could, off to where a wonderful teacher taught every day. Sometimes that was in the streets. Epictetus loved listening. He hardly noticed how cramped his lame legs grew, as he squatted on a step, or how tired he became with standing, when there was nowhere to squat.

At last, a day came when Epictetus himself was allowed to teach in the streets. He loved that. But after a while he was stopped; a new Emperor came, and many good things were changed. The Emperor Domitian would not allow any teaching in the streets, and an order went out that it was to stop.

Because Epictetus, who was an old man by this time wanted more than anything to live and teach his beautiful thoughts to others, he fled to another place, where the Emperor had no power over him. And there he set up again, and was soon happy once more teaching. He was again so happy that he almost forgot that he was lame and poor.

He lived in a funny little house that had no door – and no need of a door, because his real riches were hi thoughts, and no one could steal those. But he didn't feel poor, he felt rich.

One of his pupils wrote down some of his sayings that will never now be forgotten, and one of these was his saying about the nightingale. *If I were a nightingale*, he said, *I would pour out my song to God; but being just an old lame man, what shall I do but praise and bless Him as I am able.*

Wasn't that a lovely thing to say? Old, lame and poor — it made no difference. God would value his praises to Him! Just as he values the joyous praises of boys and girls!

Tree-Tops

It's fun to build a new house. It takes good, clever carpenters to do that, with lots of others to help them. But sometimes boys and girls build houses in trees. Have you ever seen one?

Usually boys and girls copy grown-ups; but there is a hotel in Africa called 'Tree-tops Hotel', where the grown-ups have really copied the girls and boys: because it is built right up in a tree. Long after they were grown-up, Mr Eric Walker and his wife remembered an exciting tree-house they had when they were growing up. 'Let us make a big one like it,' they said.

First, they had to find a suitable tree. After searching for a long time, they found one near to a water-hole – a giant *mugumu*, a wild fig-tree. It had fine, strong spreading branches – just right – and dark green leaves. As soon as they saw it, Mr Walker said excitedly: 'That's our tree!'

Thinking over their plans, they walked right round it. And there, in time, they had built their Tree-tops Hotel thirty-five feet above the ground (the height of six tall men). It was just right, giving them, and all who came there, a wide, high view. It had a kind of balcony, and from there they could watch the wild animals that came to the pool below to have a drink. And Tree-tops became famous as news of it spread, and lots of travellers in Africa came there to stay. One of the most special visitors was the Queen Mother, and newspapers everywhere around the world told of her visit. Later on, Princess Elizabeth and the Duke of Edinburgh were in that part of Africa, and they went to stay at Tree-tops, and saw the wild animals come to the pool below to drink. Actually, they were staying there when the news reached them that the Princess loved father, King George the Sixth, had died in London

So it was true what one writer said: 'A young girl climbed into a tree one day a Princess, and climbed down from the tree the next day a Queen.' (Because, at his death, she had to take her father's place.)

Always a list of the wild animals seen was kept – elephants and rhinos, and buffaloes, the biggest animals in the world, as they came to drink, as well as bush-buck and water-buck and monkeys and lots of others. And beautiful birds as well. How did they all get to the pool? Now this is interesting: no matter which was earliest there, they each had to give way to the biggest. (Which were the biggest? – You know.) Next came the giraffes, after them the zebras, and then the rest of the smaller creatures.

A scheme good enough for animals and birds, it seemed to be, but not for girls and boys or big people. For it isn't possible to have a happy school, a happy church, a happy city that way – with the biggest always pushing for first place. That's the jungle way, with no thought of fair shares for the smallest and weakest. Paul, who was a friend of Jesus and wrote lots of letters that are now in our New Testament, knew the proper way for girls and boys and big people. He said: *Give pride of place to one another.* (That is in the letter to his friends, printed now in Romans chapter 12, verse 10, in *The New English Bible*.) And we each know what his words mean, at home, at school, in the streets, everywhere. No pushing for first place: we are not animals, we know a better way by far!

Sorry Prayers

Big people call these 'Confessions'

Dear God, my Father for ever, I was naughty today, and it spoiled things. Please forgive me; and bring me close again to those I have disappointed. I know they love me, and You love me, whatever happens. AMEN

I was rough in my play today, dear God. Please forgive me, and let me be gentle after this. Let me share my toys and story-books, and not be selfish. Let my strong legs and arms run the messages I am asked, and play gladly. AMEN

I was rude today, dear God, and now I am sorry. Please forgive me, and remember this horrid thing no more. Let me remember always to show good manners, and to treat everyone nicely. AMEN

Dear God, I did not eat up my meal today. Mother was disappointed. She had cooked it. Now I am sorry. And when I remember that lots of boys and girls in other lands are hungry – I am even more sorry. AMEN

I was careless with my clothes today. Dear God, You have clothed well all things in Nature – the hills, the trees, the birds. Forgive me that I have not been more careful. So many boys and girls have nothing nice to wear. AMEN

Dear God, I quite forgot to give water and food to my pet today. I am very sorry. You never forget to care for my needs of drink and food. I want to do better from now on in showing my pet proper care. AMEN

God, I was impatient today, I shed tears, and would not listen properly. It spoiled things, and I am sorry now. Let laughter live in my heart, and be often on my lips, I pray, as I work and play. AMEN

Prayer Poems

Thanks be to God for our happy day,
now sun has slipped into the west,
each little bird safe in its sleep,
like friendly dogs that share our play.

With all the creatures of our world,
the kind night comes to boys and girls.
Dear God, accept our thanks, for joys
we've shared with those now snugly curled.

We've loved the wind in whirling leaves,
that is such fun to lifted kites,
with jolly swings, and bounding balls,
we bring our thanks, dear God, for these.

With little flowers here folded tight,
thanks to God for the stars on high,
in quietness and sleeping trust
and gentle darkness of the night.

Rest our bodies and sleepy eyes,
bless our bed-clothes and snug pillows,
and all our dear ones near and far,
with happy dreams till we arise.   ANON.

Lord teach a little child to pray,
    And then accept my prayer,
Thou hearest all the words I say
    For thou art everywhere.
A little sparrow cannot fall
    Unnoticed, Lord, by thee,
And though I am so young and small,
    Thou dost take care of me.
                    JANE TAYLOR, 1783–1824

Dear Lord, when we put out the light,
And all things are asleep,
Then through the velvety darkness,
Thy little children keep.   R.F.S.

Dear God –
For lovely things like growing trees,
I bring my thanks to You;
For birds, and butterflies and bees,
I bring my thanks to You.

For lovely things like flying planes,
I bring my thanks to You,
For rushing things like cars and trains,
I bring my thanks to You.   R.F.S.

Lord of the loving heart,
May mine be loving, too,
Lord of the gentle hands,
May mine be gentle, too.
Lord of the willing feet,
May mine be willing, too,
So may I grow more like to Thee
In all I say and do.   ANON.

First the seed,
And then the grain;
Thank You, God,
For sun and rain.

First the flour,
And then the bread;
Thank You, God,
That we are fed.

First Your love,
And then Your giving;
Show us, God,
Your way of living.

Thank You, God,
For all Your care
Help us all
To share and share.   LILIAN COX

God bless all friendly girls and boys
whose kindness grows each day,
who gladly share their books and toys,
and cheer us on our way.   R.F.S.

Holy God, Who madest me
And all things else to worship Thee.
Keep me fit in mind and heart,
Body and soul to take my part.
Fit to stand, and fit to run,
Fit for sorrow, fit for fun,
Fit for work and fit for play,
Fit to face life day by day.
Holy God, Who madest me,
Make me fit to worship Thee.   ANON.

Guard my lips
That I may say
Only what
Is true today.
        FIONA GLENVILLE (aged 11)

As each new day comes
with soft fall of dew,
God open my eyes
to serve You anew.   R.F.S.

Thank You, God, for daisies
that look up from the grass,
for tall trees, and rainbows
that cheer me as I pass.
And when I'm tucked-in tight,
thank You for moon and stars,
windows wide to see them,
and deep thoughts that delight.   R.F.S.

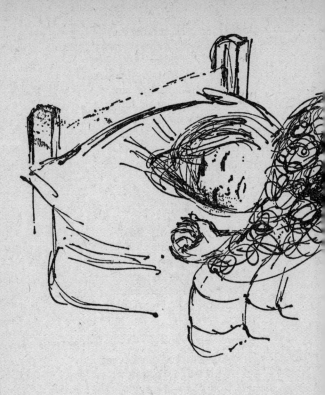

God, I'm glad that You edged the daisies with pink,
and made the forget-me-nots blue;
it's splendid to know You are able to think
of so many wonderful things to do!

That You made me, too – and only 'me',
and didn't make me Tim Brown.
And I thank You God that the hills went up
when You made the valleys go down.   SALLY COEY

Thank You, God, for winds on high,
   bringing sweetness everywhere,
For green of grass, and blue of sky,
   spelling out Your loving care.   R.F.S.

A Picnic Prayer

Dear Father, Whom I cannot see,
You are so kind and good to me;
Keep all sick girls and boys today
Who cannot come outside to play.   R.F.S.

A Sea-side Prayer

Thank You, God, for this salty air
and the sweet sunshine everywhere;
for the tide flowing in and out,
with sand for castles all about.

Here are pools to mirror my face,
with crabs and shells in every place;
here is the home of lots of fish
that hide and swim just as they wish.

Thank You, for the strength to run
upon the beach, which is such fun;
for strength to paddle, swim and float,
and all adventures in a boat. R.F.S.

God, set a smile upon my face
if things are hard in any place,
and let me play fair, this day through,
to show the love I have for You. R.F.S.

A Road Prayer

God of the glad day-time,
  and of the still, calm night,
hold us in Your keeping
  in the dark, in the light.

When we cross a wide road,
  let us look left and right
lest we should suffer hurt,
  with others out of sight.   R.F.S.

Part Three

The King's Jester

Once, there was a little 'funny man'. His name was Rahere
– R A H E R E. He lived in the Court of the King. He wore
a little red suit, with little red shoes with pointed toes,
and a little pointed cap with bells, and he knew a great
many tricks.

Noblemen and princes, as well as kings in their castles,
liked to have such a little jester to help pass the time and
keep the fun merry. They were rough days in lots of ways,
but Rahere enjoyed his life well enough in the Court of
King Henry the First.

Then suddenly, sorrow came, and everything in the
Court was changed. Even the gay heart of little Rahere
was changed. The loss of the famous White Ship and the
drowning of the Crown Prince brought sadness to King
and courtiers alike. Rahere took off his little red jester's
suit, and put on the plain brown coat tied with a rope
round his middle – the clothes of a friar, a holy man.

In a very short time little Rahere set off to Rome on a
pilgrimage – something that many good people liked to do
then. Sometimes their pilgrimages took them a long, long
way from home, and were full of dangers. Little Rahere
was not one to shirk anything, and in time he arrived in
the great city of Rome. After a little while, he fell sick
there. So sick was he, that he thought he was going to die.
Afraid, he did what many people do when they are afraid
– he prayed, and made a promise to God. He promised
that if God would make him better, and let him get home
again, he would do something for other sick people.

And at last, God heard his prayer, and little Rahere, by
degrees, got better. Lots of people, of course, forget their
promises once they are better, but little Rahere did not.
'A promise is a promise,' he said. And he was even more

eager about it when one night, in his dreams, he seemed to see a man of great strength and straightness and beauty. 'Pray, who are you?' he asked. 'I am Bartholomew, the Apostle of Jesus,' said the man of great strength and straightness and beauty, 'and I have come to help you keep your promise. When you go back to London, choose there a place in the Smooth-field. Only ask for it, and you shall receive it; seek for it, and you will find it. Have no fears about how the work is to be done – it is my work to help you.'

When little Rahere wakened, he was more than ever eager to get on with his promise. And after a long time, he stood once again in London, at the ante-room of the King's chamber. When they heard what his plan was, his old Court friends laughed at him. 'The little funny man turned serious,' they said, and thought it was the best joke of all.

But it wasn't a joke. Now that little Rahere was fit and strong, and home, he answered: 'I have business whereof I would speak with the King.' And when the King bade him draw near, he asked for that piece of ground about which he had heard in his dream.

'The Smooth-field!' said those who stood close enough to hear. 'The little man must be mad! That flat, wet, marshy place is fit only for the horses that run there, and for the hangman's gallows that stands there. It's a terrible place!'

But little Rahere went next morning to the Smooth-field, wet and waste; and people passing by laughed at his plan. The little children who played on the Smooth-field liked the little man in the plain brown coat with a rope round his middle. He played games with them, and then he asked them for their help in gathering the smooth stones that lay about. Soon, the children began to tell their fathers and mothers at home what was happening at the Smooth-field, and they, too, came to help. Little Rahere explained his plan to all who came, and soon half the people of London, it seemed, had heard about it. Courtiers

came to jeer, but they were soon struck by the honesty of the work, and the joy of those who served in it, and they left gifts of gold coins. Horse-dealers came, who held a market on the Smooth-field, and they, too, gave help as they could.

In time, the buildings rose higher and higher, until the Smooth-field was quite changed. Where there had been only wet and waste, there rose a church, a priory, and a hospital – named after St Bartholomew, whom Rahere had seen in his dream.

Little Rahere's hospital was a plain, clean place, but to the poor, sick people it seemed like Heaven – it was so full of kindness and tenderness. Soon more and more came,

and more stones and bricks were needed to make it bigger.

Little Rahere made his promise, and kept it, a long time ago – for he died in 1140 – but his work still goes on today. For there stands on part of the Smooth-field – now called Smithfield – a great hospital, Bart's, short for St Bartholomew's, the most famous hospital in all London. And nearby is the church, part of which little Rahere built himself. There he is buried.

And that's the story of the little 'funny man'.

Can you keep your promises? Little Rahere could. He said: 'A promise is a promise!' And it is, isn't it?

Timothy's Dream

Shopping in a big store is fun, isn't it? I liked shopping in Timothy Eaton's store. It is a wonderful store, the largest in Canada. And there's a wonderful story behind it.

Timothy grew up in Ireland. His home was poor, and his widowed mother had a struggle to get enough for her nine children to eat. So when he was thirteen, Timothy went to work. He found work with a merchant. It was hard work, starting early in the morning and continuing long after most boys and girls were in bed. Sometimes it was midnight before Timothy was able to crawl into his own little bed under the counter.

By the end of five years, Timothy made up his mind that he would change lots of things if ever he had a store of his own. But he had to wait a long time before this dream could come true.

Because things were so hard in Ireland, some of his brothers and sisters said 'Goodbye' and went off to Canada. And, after a time, they persuaded Timothy to join them.

The great new country was very different from Ireland and Timothy soon found work. He started in one store and then moved to another. At last – and he was thirty-five years old before the chance came – he bought a little store of his own in Toronto.

In those days shopping was very different; there were few fixed prices. It was the custom of shopkeepers to put much bigger prices on their goods than they really hoped to get, much bigger prices than they knew the things were worth. If the customers were silly enough to pay them, then the shopkeepers were well pleased. But if they set out to argue that the prices were too high, then they might be brought down a little. And sometimes the argument went on right into the night, for the shops were often still selling at midnight.

Timothy Eaton was quite sure that this was all wrong. The prices were too high, the shops kept open too long, and no one really knew by the price-tickets what a thing was to cost.

So he set about to work out his dream: a different kind of store. And he put an advertisement in the paper to say that he meant to sell goods cheaper – that he was going to sell them for cash only, not in exchange for goods, as some of the other stores did, and that the prices would be exactly what the price-tickets said. His store would open, just like the others, at eight o'clock in the morning, but it would close at six; and if anybody was dissatisfied with anything, they were to bring it back. It was all so straight-forward and fair, that it was Timothy's boast that even a child could shop in his store.

It was at first only a little store, with oil-lamps, and in the winter a little square stove. But it was quite different from any of the other stores. It was a fair and friendly place.

And it prospered. As the town grew bigger, Timothy made his store bigger. Today, it is so big that more than thirteen thousand people work in it in Toronto – and there are lots of branches in other parts of Canada.

When Timothy – grown old, making his store the right kind of store – died in 1907, one of Canada's big news-papers said: 'Mr Eaton has shown that a successful business-man can be good, clean, one might say holy. His was a beautiful life, and he will long be mourned, and never be forgotten.'

Wasn't that a wonderful thing to say?

And those who shop in his big store today, and those who worship God in the Timothy Eaton Memorial Church, remember him. Now that we have shared his story, we can all do the same.

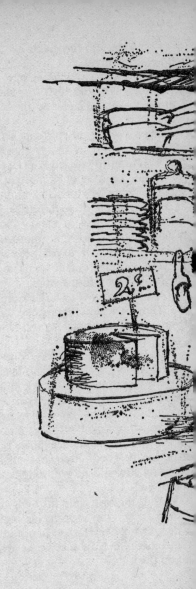

A Best Friend

Have you a dog of your very own? Not yet, perhaps. It's not as easy in the city – where there isn't much space – as it is in the country. For there are two kinds of dogs ('Lots more than two,' you say) but two *main kinds* – 'companion dogs' in the city and 'working dogs' in the country. Sir Walter Scott, a very famous writer, liked to remind us about something wonderful about both kinds. He wrote

gladly and thankfully: 'The Almighty Who gave the dog to be the *companion of our pleasures, and our toils*, has given him a wonderful nature.' And this is true of both kinds of dogs, city dogs and country dogs.

I don't know which the little boy was thinking about when he wrote his funny little poem:

> The dog is man's best friend;
> He has a tail at one end;
> Up in front he has teeth,
> And four legs underneath.

You might be able to write a better poem.

Not long ago, in New Zealand, a beautiful life-size bronze statue of one of man's best friends was put up beside the Church of the Good Shepherd, on the shore of Lake Tekapo. And it's hard to think of a nicer place in which to set that statue of a sheepdog, than on the edge of that brown-tussocked, wide-spreading sheep country. For from end to end of New Zealand there are, in all, two hundred thousand 'working dogs' – not counting city dogs. And these sheepdogs, from being tiny puppies just a few months old, are trained for just on three years. A notable trainer is Mr Broad of the Department of Agriculture, and he says something very interesting to us: 'Pups at an early age are able to tell changes of humour in the voice of their master. Most puppies can be trained and controlled only by kindness, for no other animal is endowed with a nature so affectionate, honest and loyal.' (It is nice to learn those three great gifts off by heart.) And every boy or girl who has the chance to look at – or even hear about – that monument, cast in England and now standing beside the little Church of the Good Shepherd in New Zealand, will love them.

And more than that – if any boy or girl, however small, wants to make the best of his life, and be a Christian, he or she will know that those very special things must be at the centre of his or her own life, too: *affection, honesty, loyalty!*

The Lady with the Little Cart

Let me tell you the story of a lady who had lots of friends. She lived in America, in a big city called New Orleans.

Her name was Margaret – Margaret Haughery – though no one used her full name, any more than you call your favourite sister by her full name. They called her Margaret.

When Margaret was a little baby her mother and father died; but two kind people, as poor and as kind as her parents, said she could come and live with them.

She lived with them a long, long time, until she was quite grown-up. Then she got married, and in time had a house and a little baby of her own. But before long, a dreadful sickness came to the city, and Margaret's husband and baby died.

Poor Margaret! She didn't like staying all alone in her house; she wanted to do something to help things, rather than just sit sadly at home. She went to work in a laundry in the city. It was hard work. She had to stand at a table all day long ironing the clothes that came in. Sometimes her arms ached, sometimes her back ached, and sometimes her feet ached. The nicest thing about her hard work was that her ironing-table was by a window, and when she had a minute to spare she could look out and see the boys and girls of a big Children's Home next door. When she saw those who had no fathers and mothers playing so happily, she thought of the time when she had had nowhere to go.

One day, another dreadful sickness came to the city. Many fathers and mothers died, and soon the big Home next door was nowhere near big enough for all who wanted to come into it. When Margaret heard, she was troubled. She thought and thought. At last, she came to the kind ladies who kept the Home, and said: 'I am going

to earn all the money I can, and you are to have it to make your Home still bigger.'

She set to work right away. Soon she had saved enough to buy two cows. Then she bought a little cart to drive around in the early mornings, and deliver the milk from her two cows.

Soon more customers wanted to buy their milk from Margaret's clean little cart, and she gave up going to the laundry.

She saved and saved, and bought two more cows, and got more and more customers. Then one day, she changed from being a milk-woman, to being a bread-woman instead. Still she kept her little cart, and still she gave all she could to the Children's Home.

In time, she got carpenters to build her a big steam bakery, and she got people to come and work for her. Everybody in the whole city knew Margaret by this time. The men in the shops were proud of her, the children waved to her as she came by in her little cart, and the poor people of the city came to ask her help as she sat in her office in her plain, clean working dress and shawl.

After a long, busy time, Margaret died. All the people of New Orleans then told each other what a wonderful friend she had been. And when they learned what she had caused to be written down as her last wish – or Will – they found that she had left all she had to the Children' Homes. (By this time there were several, and each got share of her savings.) Margaret hadn't been able to write out her wish for herself, because she had never been able to learn to read or write and could only sign her name with a cross. But when the people heard what her wish was, they said a lovely thing about Margaret. They said 'She was a mother to the motherless; she was a friend to those who had no friends; she had wisdom greater than schools can teach; we will never let what she has done be forgotten.'

And they didn't – they had a beautiful statue made just like she was, wearing her clean working dress, her little shawl and her sunbonnet, and sitting in a low chair, just as she did in her office when the poor people came to see her, or when she drove in her little cart. And they put her arm (in the statue) around a little child, and let her eyes look down at everyone in the kind way that they always did.

And there Margaret's statue stands to this day – the first statue ever put up in America to honour a woman. And wasn't she a lovely woman! People who knew Jesus when He lived on this earth said a wonderful thing about Him. They said: 'He went about doing good.' (Acts chapter 10, verse 38). And that was just what Margaret did. She shared Jesus's secret.

Medal from the Queen

Lots of boys and girls live in Leeds, a great bustling city in the north of England. About half a million make their homes there, and every day others of us, visitors by rail, river, canal or road, pour into the city. So there is always something going on in Leeds. Many good and useful things that we use in our homes are made by people there, including clothes, till now it is one of the largest ready-made clothing cities in the world.

A while ago fame of another kind came to Leeds, an honour which came to one who lived and worked there. Her name was Mrs Kitty Brushwood. Ever since 1907, when she was just thirteen years old, and of course, long before she married, Kitty had been a cleaner at the Carlton Barracks in Leeds, where lots of soldiers lived. Right from the first, Kitty – or perhaps we'd better call her by her proper name, Mrs Brushwood – had scrubbed mile after mile of floors, and worn out hundreds of scrubbing-brushes and mops doing it. And she had enjoyed helping to keep that huge building clean.

From 1907 to 1961 is a long time, and it seemed to those who knew the good work of Mrs Brushwood, that it was time to honour such a willing and cheerful cleaner. And do you know what they did? They wrote about her to the Queen, and the Queen sent up a medal from London the British Empire Medal, for long and faithful service to the Army, and for cheerfulness and pleasant manners that 'have endeared her to successive generations of volunteers' That's what it said in the special letter that came with it

On the great day, nearly two hundred officers and men of the Seventh Leeds Rifle Battalion, with their boots and their buttons shining, turned out on parade. The band played, and it was fitting that it should on such an exciting occasion; and Mrs Brushwood, the willing and cheerful cleaner, stood to attention to receive her medal from Major-General Lord Thurlow, on behalf of the Queen.

So now we can never think of cleaning as an unimportant job. Jesus had a lot to say about cleaning. He told about people He knew who fussed about getting the outside of things clean, but never bothered at all about the inside. Mrs Kitty Brushwood would have said at once that this is a very poor way to clean things. It's the inside that matters most. Jesus said that. Perhaps He had learned it from His mother in their little white-washed home in the village of Nazareth. When He grew up to talk to people, Jesus talked about clean cups, and clean thoughts. The Psalms that His mother helped Him to learn had something to say about clean things, too. One Psalm asked: 'Who shall ascend into the hill of the Lord, or who shall stand in His holy place?' And as quick as thought came the answer: 'He that hath *clean hands and a pure heart.*' (Psalm 24, verses 3 and 4).

So we know what to do about passing on dirty stories, mean thoughts, ugly temper. That is why someone has written a nice prayer for us each:

O God, our Father, *give me clean hands, and clean words, and clean thoughts.*

Help me to stand for the hard right against the easy wrong; save me from habits that harm.

Teach me to work as hard and play as fair in Thy sight alone as if all the world saw.

Forgive me when I am unkind, and forgive others who are unkind to me.

Keep me ready to help others at some cost to myself.

Send me chances to do a little good every day, and to grow more like Christ. AMEN

A Favourite Word

What is your favourite word?

One of the nicest in the whole world is the word
H A P P Y. Jesus used it often when He was here on earth
with people, telling them stories. He used it over and over

again, especially in what we call His 'Sermon on the Mount'. *'Happy,'* said He, *'are the kind-hearted, for they will have kindness shown to them.'* (It is printed now in Matthew's Gospel, chapter 5, verse 7, in the Phillips translation.)

One who knew this secret very well was Lyman Frank Baum, who grew up one of a big family of nine. He loved stories, and made them up; and, of course, there were always listeners in his family.

When he was twenty, and grown-up, he got married – and in time had little children of his own to whom he could tell stories. He liked that. There were four of them in the end, and one night in their simple American home, when they clamoured for a story, their father, Lyman Frank Baum, told them a new one about a little farm girl who got carried away by a great wind, to a land where she came upon a jolly scarecrow, a man made of tin, and a cowardly lion.

It all sounded fun. But no sooner had the story started, than the children spoke up to ask: 'What was the name of that land?' Quick as thought, the kind story teller looked up, and his eyes caught sight of a filing cabinet in the corner of the room, with letters of the alphabet right down it. One drawer bore the letters O–Z, and ready-made, presented him with the name he wanted. To the children, he replied: 'It was the land of Oz!' And on went the story – the happy story teller, and the happy listeners never for a moment guessing that they had added a new name to the English language.

Lyman Frank Baum seldom wrote down his stories – but this one he did. In time, he found an artist to draw him twenty-four pictures to go with it. And together they set out to find a publisher who would put story and pictures together to make a story-book for other children. At first they had a hard search; but, eventually, they found a publisher who said he would print five thousand copies. It sounded a lot, and both story teller and artist thought it would be plenty. But they were wrong: *The Wizard of Oz* – published in November 1900 – had soon all sold out. Others had to be printed. Soon, twenty-five thousand had sold; and even that wasn't enough. (By now, over five million copies of the story have been sold. And that is not all: it has been made into a movie-picture; into a long playing record; into a puppet-show, to give children happiness in that way; into a musical-comedy – for big people to see; and into a radio serial to come over the air! It has also been printed in a dozen different languages for those who don't know English. In the great country of Russia it is used in schools to teach the children English.)

And what is its secret? It's a happy story – there is no cruelty in it. Lyman Frank Baum set out, he said, 'to cut out all the horrible and blood-curdling things in many old-time fairy-tales'. *He had learned what a happy thing it is to spread happiness about the world!*

A Royal Treasure

Queen Elizabeth the Second is a Queen, dearly beloved. But no boy or girl would be so silly as to think of her as all the time sitting on her throne in the Palace. Queens used to do that – but a long time ago. You will smile at a funny little poem written about one of them:

'What a nuisance,' said the Queen,
  'I've lost my golden crown,
It must be somewhere in the place,
  Where did I put it down?'
She turned the cupboards inside out
  For half an hour or more,
And all the royal fol-de-rols
  Lay scattered on the floor.
Then suddenly she saw a mirror,
  'Dear, dear, dear,' she said.
'I never thought of looking there,
  I've got it on my head!'

Certainly that was not written about this Queen. She is not absent-minded like that – though she does live in a Palace and does have a crown. But being a modern-day Queen, she doesn't spend much time wearing it. More important to her are people, and she spends a lot of her time going about amongst them.

A while ago the Queen made a visit to a place in Africa Sierra Leone, and whilst she was there she received a lovely present. It was a Bible in the *Mende* language, and she treasured it more than ever when she heard the story behind it.

Over a hundred and twenty years ago, a ship with a deep hull and strong sails set off from the west coast o

Africa. But it was an unhappy ship, packed full of slaves, wretched African people who had been stolen away from their homes to be sold to strange masters. They knew what was ahead of them, and it filled them with fear.

But somehow – talking it all over quietly among themselves when no one was listening – they managed to revolt against their cruel Spanish masters. Securing them fast, so that they were powerless, they took charge of the ship themselves, and sailed her into New Haven, Connecticut, and threw themselves on the mercy of the American courts.

It was all very difficult – because no one there knew the Mende language. But in time, they got good Professor Gibb of the University to help them. He listened carefully, and pieced together that they had been unjustly and cruelly treated on the ship. He then placed a number of coins before them – one at a time – and got them to count them in their Mende language. Then he went round all the ships in New York harbour repeating the numbers, till he came upon a black African sailor whose eyes brightened at the sound of his own language, the Mende language. Then he got him to come and help him with the ship-load of slaves that had come.

After that, things happened quickly: the Judge in the Court heard their sad story, and decided that they must be set free from the horrid ship. Other people came forward to help them, too. They gave them clothes and beds, work to do, and schools to teach them – and above all, they told them the Good News of Jesus, and His love.

After two years, when they were asked what most they would like to do, they said that they would like to go back home. And they did – taking the Good News of Jesus and His love with them. In time, many at home became His followers, too.

At the end of a hundred and twenty years, they managed to put their Bible into their own Mende language. That was a great joy – because then they could each read all the stories of Jesus, and share them with others.

When Queen Elizabeth went on her visit to their land, they gave her as a precious present a copy of their Bible in their own Mende language, the most precious gift they had. And she carried it away home to England, with great joy – knowing that the love of Jesus is for everybody, black Africans, boys and girls and big people, and for queens, too. You can be sure that our Queen is never likely to lose that!

Joe, the Clown

Would you like to be a clown? Perhaps you would sooner be an engine-driver or a nurse. But to be a clown – a really good clown, with a pasty white forehead, a big red nose and the power to make people laugh – is a wonderful thing.

Once, there was a little boy who grew up to be a clown – the most famous of all clowns. His name was Joseph Grimaldi. Little Joe was born in London. His father was an Italian actor, seventy years old when his little boy was born. He wasn't a very kind father, or a very patient one. He used to whack little Joe very hard when he was quite small. He wanted him to be a little dancer, and to act in pantomime. And whenever Joe failed to do as his father thought he should, he whacked him hard.

But all the whackings in the world couldn't drive the laughter from little Joe's heart, and when he was nine, and his father died, he still went on acting in pantomime, and dancing. But he couldn't earn a living by that alone, and Joe had to work in his uncle's butcher's shop as well. He didn't at all like chopping up joints, and counting out sausages – he wanted to be a clown, not a butcher.

And he did become a clown – a most famous one. People came from far and near to see him, and to hear him, and laugh with him. He had – now that he was grown-up – many troubles; his young wife died, his own health gave way, and he was a cripple by the time he was forty-five. But he never let the laughter die out of his heart, and he was such a wonderful clown that people who had troubles came to love him, and went about their lives more bravely because of him.

If today you go to Holy Trinity Church, Dalston, in the east end of London, you can see a memorial to Joseph

Grimaldi, the most-loved of all the clowns. That is fitting, because Holy Trinity has been the official clowns' church since December 1959. It was dedicated by the Bishop of Stepney, at a service attended by a lot of clowns, and with a clown reading the Scripture lesson to the people in the church. Of course, he didn't have his pasty white forehead, his big red nose, and his baggy pants on that day, but still he was a clown. Even a clown has feelings and longings underneath all his fun, and he needs to hear of the love of God, told in His book, and in His church.

Close to his memorial hangs the clown's prayer, with these words beautifully printed:

O God, who has created us with the gift of laughter, we thank Thee for Thy servants the clowns. Grant, we beseech Thee, that as we fool for the sake of all Thy servants, we may become fools for Christ's sake, content to abandon all in Thy service.

That prayer is a surprise to lots of people – people who have never thought about clowns being God's servants; or have never knelt down in church, or anywhere else, to thank God for sending laughter into the world. Yet surely we should thank Him for laughter every day of our lives – laughter that is clean, and full and lively – that helps us to bear our worries, when we must, to get on with other people, and to go bravely on our way.

Helping Prayers

Dear God, I want to use my eyes and my hands to help people today. Show me how. Jesus helped in His home – carrying the water-jar, and running messages for His Mother. I want to help, too. AMEN

Help my Daddy at his work today, dear God. Help him to do it well, and to enjoy it. Help my Mummy at her work. Help her to do it well, and to enjoy it. And keep safe all who are too old and frail to work. AMEN

Dear God, help today all the people who drive buses and trains – keep them wide awake and careful. Keep the pilots who fly planes, and all who travel with them. And help the captains of the big ships. AMEN

Today, I am remembering the doctors and nurses who help You to make sick people better. Show them how to do the right thing, and let their words and hands be gentle. Jesus helped the sick people. AMEN

God, be close to all who tend babies and very tiny children today. Help them to cook their meals, and make their beds, and dress them in pretty clothes. Help them to play together with lots of fun. AMEN

O God, help all the old people to enjoy today – all who are well and happy, and all who are sick or sad. Give them good friends and neighbours to help them. And help the blind ones cross the busy roads. AMEN

Dear God, help all the children at school today to learn lots of new things, and to remember them. Help the

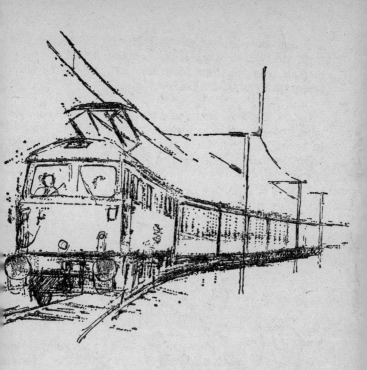

teachers – especially when they are tired; and keep the children happy at playtime. AMEN

Thank You, God, for sunny clouds that seem to make castles in the sky – and for the soft, green grass beneath. Thank You for games to play, and for sun and gentle winds that keep things fresh. AMEN

O God, I remember today all the people who have had to work while we slept in our beds. Bless the bakers, and train-drivers, and pilots of planes, and all the kind doctors and nurses and policemen. AMEN

O God, take care of the busy farmers today, and give them strength to work hard. And help all in the busy markets who sell fresh things for food, and all the shopkeepers who fill up our baskets. AMEN

O God, You have sent many people to help us whom we never see – people in factories who put good food into tins to keep fresh. Help them to keep clean, and to continue happy in their work. AMEN

Dear God, give good clear eyes, and strong bodies, to the drivers who take the big lorries to far places, with big

loads. Give them patience when cars get in their way. And bring them safely home again.   AMEN

Dear God, let boys and girls look both ways at the crossings, where the cars come. Give them patience to wait till all is clear. Save them from playing on the crossings. And help all the people who help them.   AMEN

Help mothers of little children today – to do all they can to make them clean and comfortable, and to teach them to eat and to walk and to play. Give them patience when they are tired, and love all the time.   AMEN

Dear God, help the policemen and the policewomen who work hard to keep people and things safe. Help the firemen as they dash to put out fires and to rescue people. They are all brave helpers. AMEN

Hear my prayer, O God, for all old people, and lonely people, and those who don't have nice things. I know some of them by name – but You know them all. Show me how to do something to cheer them. AMEN

God, keep safe today, and in the dark night, all the fishermen in their boats far out at sea. Keep them brave and careful – especially when storms come. Let us not waste the fish they catch for us all. AMEN

Be close, dear God, to all little children in hospital; and to all who are sick at home. Keep them snug and warm,

and give them patience to stay in bed, and to take their medicine. And help all who help them. AMEN

Bless today, Father God, all busy workers with tools who keep the parks gay with flowers, and the paths neat and tidy. Thank You for lawns, and for soft grass on which to play games. Help us each to share our joys. AMEN

Help today, dear God, all boys and girls and big people who can only get about on crutches, or with callipers, or in wheelchairs. Give them patience to keep on trying. And help the doctors and nurses and friends they have. AMEN

God, bless today all hard-working farmers, who give us the meat and butter and corn we need. Save them from

being greedy about their prices; and bless the shopkeeper:
and butchers and bakers who serve us in their shops. AMEI

Heavenly Father, help all the people who write story
books; and all who make the pictures for them. Than
You for the lovely stories told long ago and now printe
in my New Testament. AMEN

Help the builders who put up new houses for fathers and mothers and children. Let them build well, and carefully. Help the roofing-men, and the painters high up. Let the new houses be a joy to all. AMEN

Dear God, help me keep my eyes open, and be a helper, too. Save me from missing a chance — help me to care for

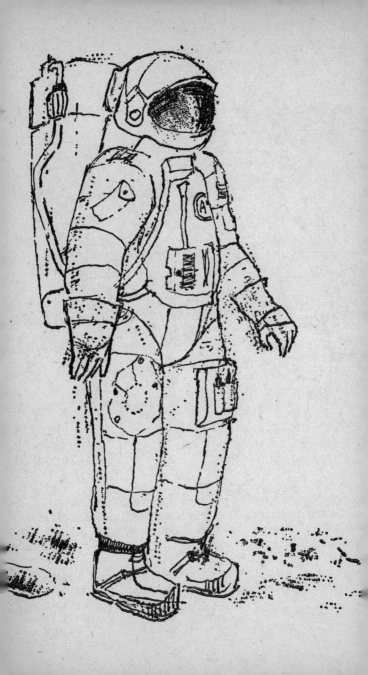

others. Let me be friendly, and kind, with a smile upon my lips. For Jesus's sake. AMEN

Give courage, dear God, to the astronauts who soar into the sky, and to the men who walk on the Moon. They have to learn a lot of hard things before they can go, and come back. Keep them safe. AMEN

O God, help all the helpers who are trying to bring peace to the countries now unhappy. Show them what to do – how to make war stop for ever. Help all children frightened by war, all hurt by it. AMEN

Give courage to Your helpers behind the scene – their work is not often praised, their paypacket is not very fat, but Your heart is gladdened by what they do. Give them happiness. AMEN

Forgive all the lazy people – especially the children who don't know the fun of helping. Jesus was Your world's best Helper – let me try to be like Him, here and now. AMEN

Acknowledgements

Among the stories specially written for this little book are some re-told in simpler language from several of my fourteen earlier books for children – reaching back nearly thirty years, and now out of print. It is nobody's fault that you boys and girls, for whom this little book has been written, missed those jolly stories – you weren't even born then.

But I hope you will be glad that I have re-told some of them, and that you will be thankful to Epworth Press for their kind permission to do so.

The pages of prayers, and the pictures, are new.

R.F.S.

The author would also like to acknowledge permission to use the following material:

In 'Shiny Shoes'
This incident is here re-told from *Portuguese Somersault* by Jan and Cora Gordon, published by George G. Harrap & Co Ltd, London, 1937.

The prayer poem on page 90 I owe to my friend Lilian Cox.

In 'Three Secrets'
This incident is based on *The Life of Alice Freeman Palmer* by George Herbert Palmer; copyright 1908 and 1924 by George Herbert Palmer; published by Houghton Mifflin Company, Boston, Massachusetts.

In 'A Little Church Mouse'
The poem about mice by Rose Fyleman is reproduced by kind permission of the Society of Authors as the literary representative of the Estate of Rose Fyleman.